CORKY TAILS
Tales of a Tailless Dog Named Sagebrush
Sagebrush and the Smoke Jumper

D1473785

Joni Franks
Illustrated by: Raquel Rodriguez

To order additional copies of this book, contact:
Xlibris
1-888-795-4274
www.Xlibris.com
Orders@Xlibris.com

This book is dedicated to Casey. Thank you for your never ending encouragement and support. And to my sweet Welsh Corgi, Sage, the most loyal, lovable dog a girl could ever have. It's been quite a journey!

Heavy black smoke hung in the crisp mountain air, and ash particles floated lightly in the breeze as a new day dawned on the cattle ranch high in the Rocky Mountains. Sagebrush, the tailless puppy, was making her way to the cow pen to help the Young Miss feed the morning grain to the hungry, bawling cattle. The Young Miss stepped outside the barn door, feed buckets in both hands, as she smelled the distant acrid smell of smoke coming from within the forest. As her eyes searched for something amiss in this otherwise perfect mountain morning, a speck of ash landed lightly on her nose. She stopped dead in her tracks as she watched Sagebrush coming toward her.

"What's that on your nose, Miss?" Sagebrush asked curiously.

The Young Miss looked toward the sky to see more ash particles now raining down upon her face. She and Sagebrush stared at each other without speaking. Suddenly, the cows began to paw at the ground, and the horses began trotting nervously and whinnying. The next thing Sagebrush and the Young Miss knew, a herd of deer came running out of the forest, straight past Sagebrush and the Young Miss.

3

"Fire!" the big antlered buck screamed as he ran across the lawn where the little mountain cabin sat. "Run for your lives! The woods are on fire!" he screamed.

The Young Miss had heard that animals in the forest have an alert system to communicate with when danger looms. The Young Miss looked wide-eyed at Sagebrush. "Go wake up your parents, Sagebrush. Hurry, we have to act fast!"

Sagebrush turned toward the cabin and began running as fast as she could to let Ginger and Maverick—her parents, the house dogs—know of the imminent danger.

"Mama, Daddy, wake up," Sagebrush squeaked as she licked the sleep from the faces of her dear parents. "I think there is a fire. Hurry! We have to go," Sagebrush continued.

"Fire?" Maverick screamed. The terrifying word loomed large in the air.

Ginger stood up, sniffing the air. "Smoke!" she screamed as the threesome went tearing out the front door of the cabin toward the anxiously awaiting Young Miss.

The penned-up livestock who were normally sweet and easy to handle had become raving lunatics, sensing something was wrong.

"Sagebrush. Go into the barn and get my wire cutters. That fire is coming this way fast."

Just then, a large smoke cloud appeared in the sky as the forest fire blew up. A hot dry wind blew in their faces. Sagebrush ran into the barn as fast as her little legs would carry her. She had to help the Young Miss. She ran straight to the toolbox, nosing through miscellaneous tools, until she found the wire cutters. Grasping them in her teeth, she ran back to where the Young Miss was waiting.

"Here they are," Sagebrush said to the Young Miss, laying the wire cutters at her owner's feet.

"What are you going to do?" Ginger cried out to the Young Miss.

"There's no time to properly evacuate the livestock," the Young Miss said to Ginger. "We are going to have to cut the barbed-wire fence. Come on. I need your help."

"What can we do?" Maverick questioned as ash debris began to stack up on his fur.

"I need you and Ginger to go and stand at opposite fence posts," the Young Miss said to Maverick. "When I cut this fence wire, I will need Sagebrush to get behind the cows and herd them to safe pasture."

As each dog assumed their positions, the young ranch woman cut the barbed-wire fence with her wire cutters. She then stretched an opening on either side wide enough for the cows to run through. Sagebrush ran to the back of the herd, nipping at the cows' heels and barking as loudly as she could, just like her owner had taught her.

The animal hooves were as loud as thunder as the dirt flew from under their feet as they raced out of the fenced area, Sagebrush running behind the herd.

Meanwhile, deep within the forest, not everyone was privy to the animals' alert system of impending danger. Some people were going about their business as they had each day.

Everyone on the ranch now knew that there were Shuns in the woods. Sagebrush had rescued two Shuns: Shroom, the old Shun, and Sprout, his young Shun son, just weeks before. The kind Young Miss had ever so generously offered Shroom and Sprout a forever home in a lovely tree hollow on her ranch. The Shuns had been so busy these past weeks with the construction of Shun Village that they had failed to inform the Young Miss that there were more Shuns just like them in the forest. The giant tree-cutting machines had made Shroom and Sprout homeless as the machines cut enormous amounts of trees from the ancient forest. Shroom and Sprout were very thankful to the Young Miss for their new home, but they weren't sure how she might feel about giving the other endangered Shuns a home as well. It was on this same fiery morning that Juniper Berry was contemplating her present situation.

Juniper Berry was a beautiful young Shun girl. Unfortunately, the giant tree-cutting machines had destroyed her and her parents' tree-hollow home. Her parents had not been quick enough to flee from the giant machines, and now Juniper Berry found herself an orphan.

Juniper Berry was so sad that she was an orphan. Her life hadn't been perfect before she lost her parents, but being an orphan was never how she envisioned her life would unfold. She remembered how she had argued with her mother and father the morning the tree-cutting machines changed her life forever. Her parents were always imposing so many silly rules upon her. They wanted her to wear dresses and be quiet and stay indoors. But Juniper Berry had other dreams besides living in a tree hole. Dresses and slippery shoes didn't suit her like her hiking boots and pants did. She liked to climb trees and explore new terrain. Lacy dresses just got caught on tree branches as she ran through the woods. She needed hiking boots so she could climb and find nuts and berries to snack on. Her mother always told her she needed to talk less and listen to others more. Juniper Berry didn't consider herself a chatty squirrel, but she did like to express her opinions when the opportunity arose. Staying inside the tree hollow like her mother wished didn't really suit her either. She loved the freedom of exploring the beautiful forest and breathing the clean, crisp mountain air. Because of her love for exploration, Juniper Berry wasn't at home in the tree hollow the day the machines came and ended up costing her everything that was familiar to her in her life.

The loss of Juniper Berry's parents was devastating. She wasn't sure what direction to turn. Thank goodness, she was a skilled gatherer. She knew where to find food in the forest. But now she was confronted with a very big problem: She needed a new tree hollow to call her home. However, that was not going to be an easy task. The giant tree-cutting machines were making it more difficult for a Shun to find a tree hollow to call their own.

And so Juniper Berry tried to go on with her life. On this morning, she knew she needed to make a genuine effort to find shelter.

Meanwhile, back at the ranch, chaos ensued. The cows, who had been released from their pen, had run to a high green pasture for safety. Thanks to the herding skills of Sagebrush and the quick thinking of the young ranchwoman, they were all safe for now.

The Young Miss dismounted from her horse as the dogs circled around her. They looked deeply into her eyes, relying on the Young Miss to provide the answers to all the questions they had in their minds. The cows had begun to settle down and gently nibble on the tall lush grass. Maverick and Ginger lay at the Miss's feet as they caught their breath from their long run.

It was Sagebrush who walked away from the group, looking up into the sky at something she had never seen before.

"Young Miss?" she asked gently. "What is that thing in the sky?"

"What in the world?" Maverick scratched his head. "Is it a giant bird?"

"That's no bird," Ginger answered as she reached for Maverick's paw. She felt like a scared wife to Maverick and a mother to Sage that had nowhere near all the correct answers for this very strange day.

The Young Miss looked to the sky, following the object with her eyes as it floated through the clouds and disappeared right at the edge of the tree line where the forest fire burned.

"It's a smoke jumper," the Young Miss stated.

"What's a smoke jumper?" Sagebrush asked curiously.

"A smoke jumper is a trained firefighter who parachutes from an airplane to fight fires in the most inaccessible remote areas of the forest," the Young Miss explained.

"Wow!" Sagebrush exclaimed, still looking up at the sky in awe.

"Smoke jumpers go to the places the other firefighters can't reach," the Young Miss continued.

"I've never heard of a smoke jumper," Maverick spoke up. "Sounds like a corky tale to me! Are you sure, Miss?"

"Yes, I'm sure. Smoke jumpers are very brave to jump from an airplane to save Mother Earth from fire," the Young Miss said.

And with that, the giant parachute and the dangling man disappeared.

Meanwhile, deep within the forest, Juniper Berry was getting tired. She had been wandering through the woods for hours, looking for tree hollows. She was just about to give up when she stumbled into an unfamiliar sight. It appeared to be a campsite. There was a fire ring where a pot of cold coffee sat. There was a small one-man tent with the flap open.

Juniper Berry took it all in. She saw a backpack sitting in the middle of the campsite. She climbed onto the open backpack, only to find a soft red flannel shirt sitting on top. She was so very tired from walking all morning that she curled up onto the soft flannel to take a little rest.

Not far from where Juniper Berry napped, the smoke jumper was busy using the skills he had been taught to contain the now-raging fire. His years of experience containing fires was paying off as he began to control the giant lapping flames. He had been at it all morning and was beginning to get very hungry. Fighting fires burns up lots of calories quickly. As he made his way to his campsite, he thought about the disturbing discovery he had made in the forest that morning.

Near the fire line where he had parachuted from the plane, he had seen one of the giant tree-cutting machines engulfed in flames. Sawdust, leaves, twigs, and pine needles from the trees had gathered in the engine motor. If this debris isn't cleaned frequently, it can become a fire hazard. The heat of the engine can easily ignite dry materials. It seemed the men driving the machines were in a hurry to cut as many trees as they could in a day and they hadn't tended to the task of cleaning the motor, causing the unnecessary forest fire. This discovery saddened the smoke jumper. If the men who drove the machines had just been more careful, this fire would not have occurred.

Pulling up his camp chair in front of the fire ring, he sat down and reached for his cold coffeepot. The discovery of the cause of the forest fire was almost as startling as what he saw next: Lying curled up on his red flannel shirt inside his backpack was the tiniest little sleeping girl he had ever seen.

Juniper Berry must have sensed his gaze upon her because she awakened at that very minute. Her first instinct was to run, but as she continued to gaze into the smoke jumper's eyes, she didn't feel scared at all.

"My name is Juniper Berry," she said softly. "Who are you?"

The smoke jumper smiled at Juniper Berry. Soot-filled laugh lines appeared at the corners of his blue-green eyes. "I'm the smoke jumper chosen to fight this forest fire. I parachuted out of an airplane this morning. I've been working to contain the fire. I was hungry and came back to my campsite for some lunch. Would you care to join me for a meal, Juniper Berry?"

Juniper Berry hadn't had a meal in a while herself. All that walking she had been doing in search of a new tree hollow had made her very hungry.

"I would be delighted to dine with you," Juniper Berry replied.

As the kind smoke jumper prepared their meal, Juniper Berry settled herself on top of the backpack and the flannel shirt where she had been napping.

"Are you out here all alone, Juniper Berry?" the smoke jumper questioned.

"I'm an orphan," Juniper Berry replied. "You see, the giant tree-cutting machines cut down my family's tree hollow. Now I am all alone. I need to find a new tree hollow to call my own. I've walked for miles this morning, Mr. Smokejumper. But so far, I haven't seen a single tree hollow. I'm going to need to travel to the deepest recesses of the forest to find one."

The smoke jumper handed Juniper Berry a plate of food, then stirred his coffee as he watched the hungry orphan girl gulp down the meal. He'd had about enough of these tree-cutting machines. It was bad enough that Juniper Berry was an orphan because of the logging of the trees. Now this forest fire had been caused by the neglect of the men who drove them.

"Do you know what a Shun is?" Juniper Berry asked between mouthfuls of food.

The smoke jumper scratched his head. "I don't believe I do, Juniper Berry."

"I'm a Shun, Mr. Smokejumper. Just like my parents before me. Our lives were once carefree because there were plenty of tree hollows to call home, as well as plenty of food to eat. Not so much anymore." Juniper Berry looked down at her now-empty plate of food. "The giant tree-cutting machines have seen to that. I'm not sure of where I am going or what I am really doing."

The kind smoke jumper felt his heart grow heavy as he listened to this sweet orphan's sad tale. "You are welcome to stay here, Juniper Berry. I have to go back and fight the fire, but you can stay here at the campsite until I get back."

Juniper Berry put down her empty plate, thinking about the kind stranger's offer. She suddenly felt very tired as she glanced at the soft flannel shirt she had been sleeping on.

The smoke jumper covered Juniper Berry with the sleeve of his flannel shirt. "You stay here and rest, Juniper Berry. I'll be back a little later, and we will have dinner together."

The thought of a hot dinner and the softness of the flannel shirt felt like heaven. Juniper Berry was sound asleep as the smoke jumper tucked her in so she wouldn't get cold.

The afternoon passed as the smoke jumper completed his duty of putting out the fire. He would spend tonight at his campsite and be picked up first thing in the morning. As he gathered his firefighter tools, he heard the bawling of cows coming from the nearby woods. He hoped they were okay. He decided he better check and make sure. Animals can get very alarmed by the threat of forest fire. Through the woods, he marched toward the bawling cattle.

As he neared a clearing where the tall thick grass remained unharmed from the fire, he peered through the trees at a very unlikely sight. The cows he had heard were peacefully grazing on tall green grass, while two cattle dogs and a tailless puppy were napping beside the herd. A woman on a horse was nearby as well.

"Hello there," he spoke as he walked toward the group. "Is everything okay?"

The lady on the horse turned to speak. "We are all fine, sir. When the fire broke out this morning, we had to move the herd to safety. I could see the flames from my ranch. It was just too close to take the chance of staying there."

"I believe I have the fire contained, Miss. It will be safe for you to move your herd back to your ranch now."

"Are you the smoke jumper?" Sage asked timidly.

"Why, yes, I am. I arrived this morning," the smoke jumper replied.

"What started the fire?" the young ranchwoman questioned.

"Unfortunately, this fire was set by the tree-cutting machines. The men who drive the machines didn't clean the debris from the motor. It may seem unlikely, but that is how this fire started. It could have been prevented."

"The tree-cutting machines again!" the young ranchwoman replied. "It's bad enough that the trees are gone from the endless cutting. Now the creatures are homeless from the cutting as well."

The smoke jumper scratched his head as he considered the question he was about to ask.

"Have you ever heard of a Shun?" he questioned the Young Miss.

It was Maverick who stepped forward to reply. "We know the Shuns. When Sagebrush first told us about them, we thought she was concocting a corky tale. But she proved us wrong. Now we have two Shuns, Shroom and Sprout, living with us at the ranch."

"Is that right?" Mr. Smokejumper replied. "I met a beautiful young orphan Shun just this morning. She's at my campsite right now. I don't know what will become of her as I am scheduled to leave here right away. Maybe you would like to meet her?" He was now speaking to the Young Miss.

"Of course," the Young Miss replied. "How far is your campsite?"

"Not far. Come on. I'll show you."

So the young ranchwoman and her dogs followed the smoke jumper through the woods to his campsite. Juniper Berry was still sleeping on top of the backpack, covered up with the sleeve of the red flannel shirt. She opened her eyes to see an entire group of dogs and people looking down at her.

"Hello, I'm Juniper Berry," she began. "Who are you?"

The young ranchwoman felt the strings of her heart pull as she looked at the little Shun girl. "Hi there, Juniper Berry. How are you?" she asked kindly.

"Not so good," Juniper Berry replied. "I have to find a new tree hollow to call home. I had one once before the tree-cutting machines destroyed the forest. I have lost my parents because of them. Now I am all alone."

Sagebrush stepped forward to speak to Juniper Berry. "Do you happen to know Shroom and Sprout? They are Shuns. I met them one fine spring day when I was strolling in the forest."

"No, I don't believe I do," Juniper Berry replied. "Are they here with you?"

"They are back at the cattle ranch," Sagebrush continued. "The kind Young Miss gave them a forever tree-hollow home on her property."

Juniper Berry looked at the young ranchwoman, thinking how lucky Shroom and Sprout were to find her. Their worries must be over now that they lived with the kind Young Miss.

"How nice for them," Juniper Berry whispered.

The young ranchwoman looked at the homeless Shun. "Juniper

Berry, would you care to see the tree hollows where Shroom and Sprout live? If you have an interest, I could see to it that you have a tree hollow of your own."

Tears were welling up in Juniper Berry's eyes. She was so tired. It would be wonderful to go with the kind lady who had so many tree hollows to offer as a home. "I would love to go to your ranch and meet Shroom and Sprout."

The young ranchwoman smiled as she picked up Juniper Berry and set her carefully on Sagebrush's back. "You ride up here on Sagebrush, Juniper Berry. Be sure and hold on tight! We've got some work to do before we go back to the ranch. We've got a herd of cows to move now that Mr. Smokejumper has made the forest safe from fire." The Young Miss smiled at the smoke jumper.

"Well, it looks like my work here is done, Young Miss." The smoke jumper smiled back. "The fire is contained, and it looks like Juniper Berry may be going to her new forever home."

"Thank you, Mr. Smokejumper," Juniper Berry cried out as she clung to Sagebrush's fur and made ready for her ride. "Goodbye!"

Juniper Berry remained on Sagebrush while the cows were herded by Maverick and Ginger and the kind Young Miss and her trusty horse all the way back to the beautiful ranch.

When Juniper Berry arrived at the cattle ranch, her eyes were wide and her fingers were tired from clinging so hard to Sagebrush's fur. Sagebrush made her way straight to the tree hollows where Shroom and Sprout were busily working.

The Young Miss dismounted her horse so she could make the proper introductions. Shroom and Sprout stopped their work, staring at the orphan girl in front of them.

"Shroom, Sprout, this is Juniper Berry," the young ranchwoman began. "We found her in the forest today while we were moving the cattle. She needs a home, just like you did. How would you feel about Juniper Berry having a tree hollow next door to you?"

Shroom and Sprout looked at Juniper Berry and smiled from ear to ear. "That would be fabulous!" Shroom exclaimed. "The more, the merrier! Besides, Shun Village can't be a real village with just the two of us."

Shroom and Sprout were so happy, they began to do summersaults in unison. Juniper Berry grinned and began doing cartwheels right alongside Shroom and Sprout in front of Shun Village.

Juniper Berry felt so relieved. She wouldn't be an orphan anymore. "Thank you all so much!" she cried.

The Young Miss looked lovingly at the Shuns as the threesome joined hands and did their happy dance.

"Well, at least one good thing came from this fire today, Juniper Berry. If it weren't for the fire, I would not have met you. And I am so very happy that I did. I want you to make yourself right at home."

Sagebrush was amazed at what all had happened on this day. As she gazed upon this happy scene, she knew that she had learned another important life lesson today. Even in the darkness of a forest fire, love and kindness won out in the end. The kind and caring smoke jumper had contained the forest fire. Shroom and Sprout had a new friend to share Shun Village with. Sagebrush felt grateful that she had Maverick and Ginger and was not an orphan like Juniper Berry. And as always, Sagebrush felt love and admiration for the kindhearted Young Miss who provided a home for them all. Even on the darkest of days, good things can happen.

Until next time!

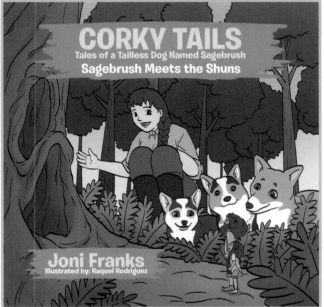

Sagebrush at the Hayden Fire Burn Scar